D0458837

Please visit our Web site at www.pelicanpub.com
for more information about these titles of
Jewish interest for children:

The Toby Belfer series by Gloria Teles Pushker:
Toby Belfer Never Had a Christmas Tree
Toby Belfer's Seder: A Passover Story Retold
Toby Belfer and the High Holy Days
A Belfer Bar Mitzvah
Toby Belfer Visits Ellis Island
and *Toby Belfer Never Had a Christmas Tree/*
Toby Belfer's Seder Audiocassette

Fate Did Not Let Me Go
By Valli Ollendorff

A Kid's Kosher Cooking Cruise
By Mildred L. Covert and Sylvia P. Gerson

ELIJAH'S TEARS

WITH ILLUSTRATIONS BY
ROSSITZA SKORTCHEVA

SYDELLE PEARL

ELIJAH'S TEARS

Stories for the Jewish Holidays

PELICAN PUBLISHING COMPANY
Gretna 2004

First published by Henry Holt and Company
Published by arrangement with the author by
        Pelican Publishing Company, Inc., 2004

---

*The word "Pelican" and the depiction of a pelican are trademarks
of Pelican Publishing Company, Inc., and are registered in the
U.S. Patent and Trademark Office.*

Library of Congress Cataloging-in-Publication Data

Pearl, Sydelle. Elijah's tears: stories for the Jewish holidays /
    by Sydelle Pearl; illustrated by Rossitza Skortcheva.
        p.   cm.
    Summary: The prophet Elijah appears in five stories about special
Jewish days, including Hanukkah, Yom Kippur, Succot, Pesach, and
Shabbat.
    1. Elijah (Biblical prophet)—Juvenile fiction. 2. Children's
stories, American. [1. Elijah (Biblical prophet)—Fiction.
2. Fasts and feasts—Judaism—Fiction. 3. Jews—Fiction. 4. Short
stories.] I. Skortcheva, Rossitza, ill. II. Title.
PZ7P31656E1   T1996   [Fic]—dc20   96-15399

ISBN 1-58980-178-4

Printed in Canada

Published by Pelican Publishing Company, Inc.
1000 Burmaster Street, Gretna, Louisiana 70053

In memory of my father, David Pearl
—S. P.
To Eli, Roumen, and Deni
—R. S.

Contents

# Preface

In the Bible, the prophet Elijah suddenly appears in the Book of 1 Kings. He is called Elijah the Tishbite, from Gilead. We don't know anything about his family life—who his parents were, what sort of childhood he had, whether or not he had brothers or sisters, or whether or not he married and had children. We do know that, as a prophet, Elijah is in communication with God. He conveys God's will to the people and challenges those who claim not to believe in God's miraculous powers.

Elijah does not die but is taken up to Heaven in a fiery chariot. He is believed to travel between the worlds of Heaven and Earth. This is thought to be a reason why he reappears in Jewish folklore again and again, usually in disguise and just in time to help someone in great distress. He is known to reward the kind and pious. Sometimes the people who are helped by Elijah do not realize it is him until he has mysteriously gone.

In Jewish tradition, Elijah is welcomed into people's homes on the seder night of Pesach, or Passover. The door is opened and a cup of wine is left for him. Elijah is thought to be present at the circumcision ceremony of each Jewish male child. He is believed to be the one who will announce the coming of the Messiah, the great redeemer of suffering for the Jewish people and, some believe, for the world. His name is mentioned in blessings and prayers, especially in the song "Eliahu Ha-Novi," which means "Elijah the Prophet" in Hebrew.

The stories in this book are associated with Shabbat, the Jewish Sabbath, and different Jewish holidays, including Yom Kippur, Succot, Hanukkah, and

Pesach. I have taken the liberty of creating Elijah's family in "Elijah's Tears" as well as Elijah's sister in "Eliora's Gifts." She shares the magical powers of her brother.

Stories about the prophet Elijah abound in Jewish folk literature. He is shrouded in magic and mystery. Some people believe that they have met or will meet Elijah during their lifetime.

Perhaps you've seen him?

ELIJAH'S TEARS

Elijah's Tears

Many years ago, when Elijah was a young man with red hair and a red beard, God spoke to him and said, "I want to know if the Jewish people are studying my Torah with a whole heart or if they are just studying it out of duty. I want you to visit synagogues all over the world. Arrive in time for Shabbat and watch the way the people care for my Torah. Come back in three months and tell me what you have learned."

And so Elijah traveled all around the world. He visited many synagogues. He was troubled by what he saw. In one synagogue, the reader read from the Torah very quickly and made many mistakes. No one corrected him! In another synagogue, the congregation didn't stand when the Torah was taken out of the ark. In another synagogue, the congregation didn't say the blessings before the reading of the Torah. In still another synagogue, the reader read from the Torah while touching each holy word with his finger instead of using the special pointer to follow along. Elijah noticed that in these synagogues, whenever the Torah was taken out of the ark, it was just a bare, uncovered scroll. And in all of these synagogues, Elijah heard no singing.

Elijah traveled from synagogue to synagogue, Shabbat to Shabbat. He ate his meals in the homes of people who invited him. He noticed that people said blessings over their food, but without joy—without a whole heart.

And so the prophet became tired and saddened by his travels. He longed to find a synagogue with people who seemed to love God and the Torah with a whole heart. He longed to find a synagogue where he could sing.

Two and a half months went by. Then one Shabbat, Elijah arrived just before sunset in a little village where the people seemed to be rushing to the synagogue with great smiles on their faces. Elijah thought he heard melodies in the air. He went to synagogue that night and felt the joyful way that people greeted each other. "Shabbat Shalom! Shabbat Shalom!" A young man with a child in his arms invited Elijah to come and stay for Shabbat.

That Shabbos morning, in the synagogue, Elijah watched as the same young father and his child opened the door of the ark together. The Torah was covered with a tallis. The people passed the Torah around and hugged and kissed it as they sang. They seemed to love the Torah with a whole heart.

Elijah loved that synagogue. He stayed for the next Shabbat and the next Shabbat and the next. Elijah stayed in that little village and became a baker. He looked forward to Shabbat, when the people would eat the challot that he baked. Elijah loved to go to the synagogue and listen to the Torah being read. He especially loved to read from the Torah himself. Most of all, he loved to sing Shabbat songs.

Elijah met a young woman in that little village and he grew to love her. Her name was Devorah. They married and had a little daughter, Penina, which means "pearl." Elijah was busy with his family, his job as a baker, and attending his synagogue. He forgot about God's request of him! And so the years passed . . .

One Shabbat, a stranger, a young woman with long brown hair and a long white dress, came to the synagogue. Elijah noticed that she wore a white string around her neck like a necklace. After services, Elijah invited her to share the Shabbat meal at the table of his family. The woman accepted his invitation. After the meal, Devorah and Penina went to sleep, while the young woman stayed with Elijah at the table and studied the Torah and sang song after song with him. Elijah, who loved to study the Torah and loved to sing, didn't want to stop. The woman knew every song that Elijah knew, and she even taught him new songs.

"You remind me of the people who pray at your synagogue—you pray with your whole heart," the young woman said.

It was then that Elijah remembered God's request. God had said, "Watch the way the people care for my Torah. Come back in three months and tell me what you have learned."

Elijah thought to himself, "Three *years* have gone by. God will surely be angry with me!"

And Elijah began to cry in his fear.

The young woman spoke to Elijah: "Don't be frightened. I am a messenger from God. Elijah, you have found a synagogue that loves God and the Torah. You stayed here because of this love. God is not angry. You must bring this synagogue a gift."

Elijah, his tear-streaked face between his hands, looked up at this woman. On the string around her neck were ten glistening pearls where there had once been just a white string. The young woman fingered them.

"These are the tears you have just shed." She took off one of the pearls and gave it to Elijah. "Take this and place it on top of the Torah of your beloved synagogue. The Torah shall wear the pearl like a crown. Your task for the rest of your life will be to find synagogues where people love the Torah with all their hearts. Find nine more of these synagogues and upon each of their Torahs you will place a crown of one of these pearls."

And she took off her necklace with the nine pearls that were left and gave it to Elijah. It glowed in his hands. "When there are no more pearls on the necklace, it will be then that Mashiach, the Messiah, will come."

The messenger continued: "You may stay with your beloved family and synagogue during the year but you must travel to synagogues all over the world at Pesach time. People will open up their homes to

you on the seder nights so that you may eat and drink and rest from your wanderings."

❖

It is said that Elijah is an old man now. His red hair and beard have turned white. He is still searching for the other nine synagogues where he may place each of the remaining pearls.

The next time you are in a synagogue, check the crown of the Torah carefully. Perhaps you'll see one of the tears of Elijah—one of the messenger's pearls.

Leaves

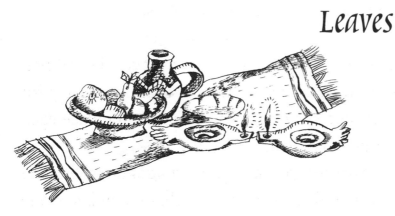

Once, in the springtime, an old man and an old woman moved from one small village in Poland to another. When their new neighbors came to visit, they noticed their beautiful golden Shabbat candlesticks were in the shape of leaves. The neighbors asked the old man and the old woman to tell the story of those candlesticks. The old couple said that they would tell the story the next autumn, when the leaves fell from the trees.

That autumn, during the holiday of Succot, the old woman and the old man invited their neighbors to their succah, their little outdoor hut, for the third meal on Shabbat. After they had eaten, the man picked up the candlesticks and brought them to the table. The old woman began to tell the story.

She said that years ago, when they were young and newly married, they were very poor. Both she and her husband were tailors, but they couldn't find work. They were religious and always looked forward to celebrating Shabbat. They loved to light the candles and to sing Shabbat songs. They especially liked to make Havdalah and sing the song "Eliahu Ha-Novi."

But after a while, they had nearly run out of money—and still neither of them could find work. They soon realized that they would only be able to celebrate one more Shabbat with wine, challot, enough food, and candles. They would have to sell their silver candlesticks. They had no choice—what else could they do?

That Shabbat, they lit the candles and said the blessing. They ate the good, simple food the woman had prepared. Then they went to synagogue and prayed very hard that they would find work by some miracle so that they could continue to celebrate Shabbat.

As they were leaving the synagogue, they noticed a stranger with a long white beard and a black yarmulke upon his head. He had a wrinkled face but a very straight back, like that of a young man. He was wearing a torn coat, pants with holes in them, socks torn at the heel, and sandals. In his arms, he carried an old siddur.

The man and the woman looked at each other and thought the same thing. They thought that they could help this man!

When they went out of the synagogue, they waited for the other people to walk past. Then they approached the old man, who was walking slowly in his sandals. He was reading from his old siddur. They went up to him and tapped him on the shoulder. He paused, placing his finger on a word in the prayer book. They noticed that his shirt had big holes where the buttons used to be.

"Excuse me," said the man, "but you see, I am a tailor and so is my wife. I would like to sew your coat."

"And I would like to mend your socks and fix the holes in your pants and shirt," added his wife.

"But I cannot pay you," replied the stranger. He turned his pockets inside out—they were filled with holes.

"We won't be any richer or poorer for doing a mitzvah," said the man and woman.

"But these are the only clothes I have," said the stranger.

"Listen," said the man. "Come to our house after Shabbat. We will sew your clothes. Then, while we sew, you may rest under the cover of our bed so that you'll stay warm."

The stranger agreed to come to their house after Shabbat.

The couple walked to their home feeling very happy that they'd be able to help the stranger before the weather turned colder.

At the end of Shabbat, they made Havdalah and sang "Eliahu Ha-Novi." It seemed that immediately after the song was over, there was a knock at the door. They went to answer it. It was raining very hard outside.

The stranger stood in the doorway. Raindrops were sliding down his face. The man and woman motioned for him to come into the house. They noticed that his clothes were not wet at all and the old siddur he carried was completely dry! They let him rest in their bed under the cover and gave him some tea to drink (it was all that they could offer him); then they got to work. They stayed up most of the night and sewed and sewed the stranger's clothes until they had finished. The husband and wife slept on the rug near the fireplace because they didn't want to awaken the stranger who had fallen asleep in their bed.

In the morning, they gave the stranger his newly mended clothes. There were no more holes—not even in the pockets of his coat.

The stranger dressed and thanked the man and woman.

"You will be blessed," said the stranger before he left.

The next day the husband and wife took the candlesticks to the marketplace and sold them. They bought food with the money. The following Friday came quickly. That morning, the husband said to his wife, "Let us take a walk into the forest to see the trees with their beautiful leaves. We will celebrate Shabbat in our own way. God will know of our observance."

Together they started out. They walked deep into the forest near their house. As they walked, they held hands and looked about them at the beautiful colors of the autumn leaves. Suddenly, they noticed leaves shining in the sunlight up ahead. They ran to the leaves and picked them up. They seemed to be made of gold! Then they became aware of a man walking slowly in front of them. His head was bent as though he were reading a book, and each time he made a footprint a golden leaf fell inside of it! The man and the woman picked up all the golden leaves that they could carry—all of the leaves that had landed in the old man's footsteps. They ran to the man, holding out the leaves and explaining that he must have dropped them. When the man looked up from his book, they saw that it was an old siddur. They noticed his clothes and his long white beard—he was the stranger whose clothes they had mended!

"I am praying," the stranger said. "You mustn't interrupt my prayers."

"But these are your leaves!" the couple insisted.

The stranger looked surprised.

"*My* leaves? Why, no! Do they not come from the tree—the tree of life?"

And then the stranger opened up his old siddur and turned to a page. He mumbled a prayer and then looked up. Golden leaves fell down like rain from the tree above them.

The husband and wife looked up at the cascading

leaves in wonder, and when they looked down again the stranger had disappeared.

The old siddur remained. It was opened and there were two leaves upon the pages.

"Let us gather these golden leaves. They are meant for us!" said the wife. "Now we can celebrate Shabbat!" And she began to cry.

Two tears fell—one from each eye—and landed upon each leaf on the open pages of the prayer book. Miraculously, they became candlesticks in the shape of leaves!

The husband and wife quickly picked up their new candlesticks, all of the golden leaves they could carry, and the old siddur. They hurried through the forest until they arrived in town. There they bought wine, challot, candles for their new candlesticks, and fruits and vegetables to eat, all for their celebration of Shabbat.

❖

"We're very old now," the husband and wife said to their neighbors. "But we will always remember that wonderful Shabbat. As it happened, we had gathered enough golden leaves to last us all our lives! And we have never forgotten the stranger who visited us in our time of need. We think it was Elijah."

And when the voices around the table joined in with the song "Eliahu Ha-Novi" at Havdalah, a strong sudden wind seemed to rustle the pages of the old siddur. Two autumn leaves the color of gold found their way inside the succah and fell upon the pages of the old siddur. It was then that they all knew that the prophet Elijah, Eliahu Ha-Novi himself, had been listening to the story!

Eliora's Gifts

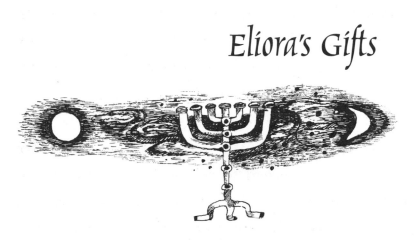

Eliora, Elijah's sister, was a weaver. She wove tallises out of the wind as she sat at her loom overlooking her garden. She kept a Torah on the small table beside her and would study it before she gathered strands of wind to weave for each new piece. As she wove, sometimes her long, wavy brown hair became entangled in the threads of wind that she grasped between her fingers. The dresses that she wove for herself to wear for each season looked very much like her tallises. In the spring and summer, her tallises often shimmered from the sunlight and flower petals that were carried in the threads of gentle winds.

Sometimes her tallises carried silver droplets from the rain that fell while Eliora wove. In the autumn, she wove tallises from stronger strands of wind sprinkled with the colors of the changing leaves. In the winter, her tallises were made from fervent winds that sometimes carried snow with them.

In Hebrew, Eliora's name means "my God is light." She indeed carried a light and a warmth within her, and it showed in her eyes. One day, as she sat weaving near her garden, God told her that it would be her task to bring light to the people who needed it most. "But how will I know who is in need of light? And how shall I bring light to them?" Eliora asked God. "You will know," said God, "when you look into the eyes of people. You will bring them light by helping them to see beauty."

And so Eliora paused in her weaving. "If I am to bring light to people I must be sure that I can see and feel the light myself," she thought. She began to take long walks. She woke up very early, when it was still dark, and she walked into the light of the sunrise, her long dress billowing in the wind. She walked all day, into the sunset and into the moonlight. She slept in open fields, under the shelter of doorways, in the homes of people that she met—wherever she found herself. She was never too cold, too warm, too wet, or too frightened—God watched over her as she slept.

One morning she awoke to the call of wild geese and found herself in a field where the geese were sucking dew from the grass. One morning she awoke under the doorway of a store and saw above her the silver threads of a spider's web glistening with raindrops that had fallen in the night. One morning she awoke to the sound of waves against the rocks. One morning she woke near a snow-covered tree in a city park and saw an old woman reaching into her tattered pockets to feed crumbs to the birds.

Eliora felt a new wonder enter into her eyes. She walked for a year, feeling the light of the sun all over her body, especially in her hands. She felt the long, expansive rays of light in the summer; she felt the dappled, mournful light of the autumn that hinted at

23

the impending darkness to come; she felt the short hours of light in the winter that seemed to slip through her fingers; and she felt the light growing around her and within her with the approach of spring. She walked to cities and she walked to towns. She walked all over the world, noticing the people who passed by her. She peeked through the windows of houses, schools, hospitals, and nursing homes.

When she looked into people's eyes, she often saw that they were tired, hollow, and sad. But she always sensed a spark of light in their eyes, deep down, behind the lids. She noticed that in the wintertime the eyes and faces of the people seemed to be dark and empty. Eliora decided to weave gifts for the people to help them get through the cold winter. She decided to give her gifts away in time for Hanukkah, the Festival of Lights. After all that walking, she felt very tired and yet filled with an energy to return to her loom.

It was springtime when Eliora once again sat at her loom overlooking her garden. The flowers were

24

blooming so beautifully and the birds were singing so sweetly, it was as though they were welcoming her home. Eliora reached for the strands of wind to place in her loom and she felt filled with a great love for the people she had seen in her travels. "I have woven enough tallises to give away to people in synagogues. I must weave other things to bring the light to people in their homes or wherever they need it most," she thought.

Eliora remembered the way the sunlight felt on her body and how it looked in the sky. She remembered the call of wild geese, the spider's web glistening, the waves rolling against the rocks, and the tenderness of the old woman feeding the birds on a winter morning. She thought of the eyes of the people that she had peered at from the windows of houses, schools, hospitals, and nursing homes. Eliora wrapped one of her tallises around herself and prayed that her fingers would be able to capture the light and the beauty that she had seen on her journey. Then she began to weave with an eagerness she had never felt before.

Even the birds that lived in her garden paused in their singing to watch her.

All through the spring, summer, and fall, Eliora wove tablecloths, challah covers, curtains, and blankets out of the wind. Raindrops, flower petals, grasses from open fields, sand from the sea, the feathers of birds, and the light from sunrises and sunsets filled her weaving with great light and beauty. Eliora was very tired from so much work, but she did not rest because she still had many gifts to make before Hanukkah.

After the first snowfall, Eliora began to weave gloves out of snow. As she wove, she remembered the light of the sun, the moon, and the spark that flickered in the eyes of each person that she had seen. She wove as many gloves as she could before the first night of Hanukkah. When Eliora tried on a pair in the dark, she discovered that they lit up her fingers like candles, and when she held up her gloves, palms facing outward, the gloves looked like a menorah! She knew that children especially would love to receive this gift.

On each night of Hanukkah, Eliora would say the blessing over the candles, and then she would travel around the world and give her gifts away. On the first night, she left piles of her tallises in synagogue sanctuaries. On the second night, she left tablecloths for the people in the different homes that she had seen through the many windows she had passed on her journey. On the third night, she left challah covers for them; on the fourth night she left them curtains. On the fifth night, she traveled to homes of children all over the world and left them blankets. On the sixth night, she traveled to hospitals all over the world and gently covered the sleeping patients with her blankets. On the seventh night, she traveled to nursing homes all over the world and covered the old people with her blankets. On the eighth night, she traveled to schoolyards all over the world and left many pairs of her glove menorahs for the children to find, keep, and give away to those who needed them most.

When Eliora returned to her home on the eighth night, she was so tired that she could barely move.

For a month she was sick and needed to rest. When she couldn't sleep, she covered herself with her own blanket made from woven images of water, sun, birds, and flowers, and she felt better. When she wore her glove menorah, the bright lights cheered her and helped her to forget that she was ill. Eliora longed to see the people who received her gifts.

Finally, when she felt strong enough, Eliora began to walk to visit with the people. First she visited the hospitals and nursing homes. When she passed by the different rooms, people waved and smiled at her. They knew she was the one who had given them the blankets because her dress glowed with a similar light. They thanked her, and she saw that their eyes were bright. She visited the houses where she had left her gifts of tablecloths, challah covers, and curtains. She visited the synagogues where she had left piles of her tallises. Eliora marveled at the light and beauty of her own work and the brightness of the eyes and the smiles of the people who greeted her.

It was the sight of the glove menorahs that touched Eliora the most. She saw them everywhere she walked. They shone on the hands of the children and their families, the hands of the homeless people who passed her with their carts and plastic bags, and the old people who walked by and waved. The eyes of the people were almost as bright as the glove menorahs that they wore!

And wherever Eliora walked, she could see her glove menorahs hanging from the branches of the trees. She knew that children became worried that the trees were cold in the winter winds without their leaves. They threw some pairs of the glove menorahs up to the trees and they became stuck on the branches. Eliora could see birds fly by wearing her glove menorahs on their wings! She knew that the children also gave some of her glove menorahs to the birds to provide them with extra warmth. Eliora returned to her home feeling so happy that the light within her seemed even brighter than before.

❖

All this happened many years ago. Eliora is an old woman now. Her long, wavy brown hair has turned white, though her face carries no wrinkles. She is too weak to weave all of the things she used to on her loom. Now she rests in the spring, summer, and fall. She watches the light of many sunrises and sunsets. She remembers that wonderful year when she traveled around the world and met many people and gave them many gifts.

Every winter, after the first snowfall, Eliora gets to work at her loom. She weaves as many glove menorahs as she can. Each Hanukkah, on the first night, she says the blessings over the candles, and then she gathers all of her glove menorahs into a big pile. She travels to a schoolyard somewhere in the world and leaves pairs of her glove menorahs for the children to find, keep, and give away to those who need them most.

After the first night of Hanukkah, look carefully in

your schoolyard. Perhaps you will see Eliora's glove menorahs. Look for them hanging from the trees as you pass along your way. Look for birds wearing glove menorahs on their wings. Look for glove menorahs on the hands of the children and grownups that you meet. Notice the light in their eyes.

The Tallis

Once there was a boy whose mother suddenly died when he was very small, leaving his father alone to care for him. The father, who was religious, became so sad and angry that he could no longer pray, and so he took his yarmulke and his tallis and hid them in the bottom drawer of his dresser. He raised his son in the best way that he knew how. He worked very hard and was often very tired.

One autumn, when his son was about four years old, the changing colors of the leaves made the man long to grasp his tallis and put it around his shoulders and to touch his yarmulke and place it lovingly upon

33

his head. He went to the bottom drawer of his dresser and reached for them. But as soon as he gazed upon them, the sadness and the anger that had filled him when his wife died came over him and he could not put them on.

The next year, when the boy was five, the leaves were changing color once again. As the boy gazed out the window, he noticed that people were walking in their best clothes along the big avenue. They were walking with such a purpose that the boy pondered this and asked his father: "Papa, why are all those people dressed up? Where are they going?"

And his father, who used to be one of those people dressed so nicely on his way to synagogue to pray, remembered. He remembered that it was Yom Kippur, the Day of Atonement. And he thought, "My son does not know anything about the heritage of his people."

He said to his son, "Come here." Together they went into his room, and he opened the bottom drawer of the dresser. The father pulled out his wrinkled tallis and yarmulke. He put the yarmulke upon his head and wrapped the tallis around his shoulders. Then he drew his son into its folds.

It was time to go to synagogue. And so they went, wearing their finest clothes. As they walked on this holy day, the father talked softly to his son about being a Jew, about the meaning of Yom Kippur, about what a synagogue was, about why he wore a tallis and a yarmulke.

When they got to the synagogue in the midafternoon, the boy was struck by all the people, the silence when the rabbi spoke, the swaying and the singing. But most of all, the father could see that the boy loved the tallis. During the service, the father slipped the tallis off of his own shoulders and rested it upon the shoulders of his son. And his son hugged it to him and prayed in his own way. The boy loved it so much that he wanted to sleep with it, and so his father let him.

From then on, the two of them would go to synagogue sometimes on Friday nights and Saturday mornings for the Shabbat service. The father felt much more at peace now that he was able to pray again. He took great pride in the way his son so quickly learned the Hebrew.

The father decided to give the tallis to his son. He called his son to him one night when the leaves began to gather on the ground just before the next Yom Kippur.

"My son," he said, "just as my father gave to me this tallis, I give this tallis to you. I know that you have come to love it." Inside the fold of the tallis, the father showed the boy where he had written: "To my dear, dear son—with much love, from your father." The boy happily slept with the gift wrapped tightly around him. In the morning, he said, "Papa, I would like to put a prayer in this tallis." He told his father what he wanted to say, and his father wrote: "I pray that my father won't have to work so hard, so that we can have more time to be together."

They went to the synagogue that Yom Kippur, and

the boy hugged his tallis to him. As they were leaving along with the crowd of worshipers, the boy noticed an old man who seemed to be waiting near the side of the synagogue. His clothes were ragged and he had no shoes, but he smiled at the boy, and the boy smiled back at him.

"Shana tova," said the boy as he held his father's hand. "Happy New Year."

And it so happened that the old man's face stayed with the boy. He wondered how he was. Every time that he went with his father to the synagogue for the Sabbath service, he would look for him. But he never did see him.

The next Yom Kippur, when the boy was seven, he wanted very much to give something to the old man who waited outside of the synagogue. "Maybe he will be hungry," he thought. He took an apple and put it in his pocket. Before the service, he asked his father to write a prayer in the tallis. The prayer was: "I hope that the man who waits near the synagogue will not be hungry this year." In the morning, the boy wrapped his tallis around his shoulders and walked with his father to the synagogue.

After the service, as they were leaving the synagogue, the boy saw the old man—the very same man he saw last year. He looked into the old man's face, which seemed a bit dirtier than he remembered and a bit more wrinkled. He gave the man the apple and said, "Shana tova—Happy New Year." The man took the apple and they smiled at each other.

The boy continued to go to the synagogue, to sleep with his tallis, and to pray. He wrote a prayer himself inside the fold of the tallis before the next Yom Kippur: "I pray that the man who waits near the synagogue will not be cold or lonely this year."

On Yom Kippur, the boy and his father walked out of the synagogue. The boy saw the man waiting in his usual place. The man did not smile this time. He was stooped. He looked old and sad. He looked sick. The boy dropped his father's hand and walked toward the old man. The boy thought, as he hugged his tallis to him, "This man needs this tallis." He let the tallis slide off of his shoulders and he put it about the trembling shoulders of the man.

"Shana tova," the boy said. "Happy New Year." The old man hugged the tallis to him. Then the boy and his father walked toward home. And as they walked, it occurred to the boy that he had given away the tallis that he dearly loved, the tallis with the prayers inside of it, the tallis that once belonged to his father. The boy began to cry. "What's wrong?" asked his father. And the child explained through his tears.

"Well," said his father, "you gave a present to someone who needed it. It is a mitzvah, my son." And they continued on their journey.

When it came time to go to bed, the boy who had slept with his tallis for years had trouble falling asleep. His father awoke to his cries and saw him sitting on the couch with a blanket wrapped about him the way he used to wrap the tallis about him—only it was not the same.

"You are sad because of the tallis. You are sad because you no longer have it. Come," said the father. "Let us go outside. There is something I want to show you."

They stepped outside into the moonlight and looked up. There were all those stars!

"Look," said his father. "This is a tallis. This is God's tallis. We always have this tallis whenever we feel alone. We have only to look up to the stars and we will see God's tallis in the sky."

The boy felt comforted. He went to sleep, grasping the blanket around him and dreaming of the old man wrapped in his tallis in the sky.

And now, instead of hugging his tallis, the boy gripped his father's hand when they prayed. At night, before he went to sleep, the boy often looked up at the sky and thought of his tallis and the old man.

❖

The years passed. The boy still thought of the old man, though he did not speak of him. He refused to wear another tallis—he had too many memories of the tallis that he used to write his prayers in and sleep with like a cover.

"Now the sky is my tallis," he'd say. He took comfort in looking up at the stars that seemed to envelop him at night.

When the boy turned thirteen and was ready for his bar mitzvah, he walked with his father to the synagogue, but he did not hold his father's hand. His eyes rested for a moment—as they usually did—outside the synagogue where the old man used to wait.

Before they went inside, the father gave his son a new yarmulke and kissed him. The father thought of his beloved wife, who would have been so proud of their son.

The boy wore his new yarmulke but he wore no tallis, as was his custom. Before his haftarah, he found himself telling the story of the tallis that he loved but gave away.

"I have never seen the old man again, nor have I seen the tallis. But I'll always remember the story and I wanted to share it with you."

The congregation listened to him intently, moved by his words.

When the boy went to the bookshelf to return his prayer book, he was surprised to find a folded paper bag sitting on one of the chairs of the sanctuary. It seemed to belong to no one and no one could remember having seen it.

The boy opened up the paper bag, and there was his tallis! The congregation stopped eating and talking and watched him. The boy hugged the tallis to him and read aloud each of the prayers that he and his father had written in its folds. To his surprise, he found a new one written with silver thread that said:

To the boy who showed me such kindness when I needed it most. I give to you my blessing. Shana tova vi chaim tovim. A good year and a good life. I pray that you will not be hungry, cold, or lonely.

—Elijah the Prophet

Tears fell from the boy's eyes, and in the blur he caught sight of something shiny peeking out from one of the folds. It was silver and slippery and strangely cold to the touch. It clung to the tallis. The people who had gathered around the boy gasped. It was a star!

That night, when the boy prayed, he noticed that the star was gone. "It has returned to the sky," he thought.

But it came back to his tallis in time for the morning prayers. And all of his blessed life, the boy prayed under his tallis in the light of the day and under the stars of God's tallis at night.

Joseph the Potter

Joseph was a potter who lived alone in the city of Haifa. In the beginning, his work was filled with a great joy and he would finger his clay lovingly. Then, as he grew older, he could not mold the clay the way he wished to, and he thought that there was something wrong with his hands.

One day, Joseph closed his shop and traveled by bus to the city of Jerusalem. He walked to the kotel, the Western Wall, on a Thursday afternoon. He saw many people praying—men on one side and women on the other. He heard yeshiva students singing. He noticed how the Wall was overflowing with paper prayers. Joseph decided to write his own prayer. With a pen and a scrap of paper that he found in his smock, he wrote, "I am Joseph the Potter. There seems to be something wrong with my hands. I wish to find great joy in my work as I once did. Please help me." Then Joseph folded his scrap of paper carefully and stuck it into a tiny crack of the Wall. Joseph stayed at the Wall for a long time watching the people pray. When each person left, Joseph touched the stones that they had touched. Sometimes the stones were wet where tears had fallen. Joseph stood at the Wall with his eyes closed, touching the stones and gathering the dust and the tears on his fingers. He was aware of a great joy that engulfed his whole body and settled in his hands.

Then he became aware of a voice speaking softly behind him. "Excuse me. Sleecha." Joseph turned around and saw an old man with a cane. His eyes were closed. "Could you help a blind man write a prayer to slip into a crack of the Wall?"

"Of course," said Joseph, blinking his eyes and fumbling in his smock for another scrap of paper and the pen. "What is your prayer?"

"I wish to meet someone who can make me the thing from my childhood that I have lost but never forgotten. When I hold it in my hands, I will believe in magic once again."

Joseph's hand trembled with excitement as he wrote the man's prayer. Then he folded it carefully and slipped it into a crack of the Wall.

"I am Joseph the Potter, from Haifa," he said, holding out his hand for the old man to shake. The old man grasped Joseph's fingers, which were resonating with the feel of the stones and the tears.

"Your hand is filled with the mystery of prayer," the old man said. "Put your hand upon my face so that you may feel my wrinkles and so that I may feel your strength."

Joseph put both hands upon the wrinkled face before him. He felt that he was gathering Time upon his fingers and he held his breath.

"Now you carry the mystery of prayer and the mystery of time in your hands. You are the one to make me the memory from my childhood. Meet me here in this spot on Pesach and bring it to me. I will be waiting with great anticipation. . . ."

Then Joseph watched with wide eyes as the old blind man turned around and walked slowly away, leaning on his cane. Soon he disappeared.

Joseph traveled back to Haifa on the last bus of the day. He looked out of the window and didn't see the trees, people, or cars that passed by. He was filled with the spirit of the old blind man. His eyes seemed to have lost their ability to see, while his hands ached to hold the clay and feel it between his fingers.

That night, on the bus ride home, it rained. Joseph could hear the rain singing softly, "Pesach is in a month and a day . . . a month and a day . . . a month and a day. . . ."

Joseph went into his little house trembling. He went right to the room that he used as his workshop and began to touch the clay and mold it with his fingers. The block of clay felt as if it were on fire, and he suddenly dropped it! When he touched it again, it appeared to be beating on its own with a steady heartbeat! Joseph held the clay in his hands and let his head fall against his chest. The lulling rhythm of the beating clay seemed to say, "Pesach is in a month and a day . . . a month and a day . . . a month and a day. . . ." Joseph fell asleep and started to dream.

He dreamt that he met a little boy who was crying, his hands cupped over his eyes. "What is it?" asked Joseph. The tears of the boy slipped between his fingers, and Joseph caught them in his hands. The little boy took his hands away from his eyes and kept his eyes closed. He was blind. "I lost something and I want it back!"

"What did you lose?" Joseph asked. He looked for the little boy and couldn't find him. He had disappeared. Then Joseph woke up.

As time passed, Joseph found that he was very busy in his workshop. Something had happened to

49

his hands—they were full of life! He felt deeply satisfied with the bowls and cups he made. People told him that their food and drink had never tasted so good. Could he please make them another bowl? Another cup? From all over Haifa, people came to ask for his business. From Tel Aviv they came. From Jerusalem they came. Even the kibbutzim contacted him and asked for his special cups and bowls.

Joseph was very happy, because the great joy that he had once felt about his work came back to him. His face glowed with a soft light and his eyes and his smile were bright. Only one thing puzzled and troubled him. It was the thing that the old blind man expected him to make. The time was passing rapidly, and there were only two more weeks until Pesach. Every night he dreamt about the little blind boy who cried and asked for the thing he had lost. Every night Joseph woke up discovering that his fingers were wet from catching the tears of the boy. He wondered what the dream meant.

One day before Pesach, Joseph closed up his shop. He sat at his bench and molded the clay. He thought of the little boy from his dreams. The clay in his hands was burning like fire, and he dropped it! Then the clay felt like it was beating with its own heartbeat! Joseph remembered the old man's words: "Now you carry the mystery of prayer and the mystery of time in your hands. You are the one to make me the memory from my childhood. . . ."

With his eyes closed, Joseph shaped the clay slowly, as though searching for the body to carry the tiny heart. The wrinkles of the old man's face, the tears from the Wall, the tears from the little boy of his dreams, and the touch of dust from the stones where the people had prayed at the Wall echoed in his fingers. The clay became very soft and fuzzy in his hands. A gentle wind blew against his fingers and he felt the tiny heart beat faster. Joseph opened his eyes in astonishment and saw a small white clay bird in his hands, beating its stone wings and looking at him with big eyes. And Joseph was afraid. He was afraid of the power that had come into his hands. He wished to see the old blind man as quickly as possible and be rid of the bird.

That night he slept fitfully. This time, when the little dream boy cried out for the thing he had lost, Joseph reached for the bird and gave it to him. The little boy held it in his hands and kissed it. The bird struggled and tried to fly away. Joseph took the bird out of the little boy's hand.

"You are the old blind man that I met that day at the Wall. I will give you the bird tomorrow."

The little boy smiled and Joseph saw his face age suddenly. His voice sounded old when he whispered, "I can wait, Joseph the Potter. I can wait."

Early in the morning on the day of Pesach, Joseph traveled to Jerusalem by bus. He held the little clay bird with the stone feathers on his lap with restless hands.

At the Wall, Joseph walked facing the prayers in the cracks and looked for the old blind man. There he was, leaning on his cane with one hand while the other hand was outstretched. Joseph placed the little clay bird with the stone feathers into his wrinkled hand. The feathers rustled, and the old blind man dropped his cane and soothed the bird with his other hand. His eyes were wet.

"This is like the bird I played with when I was a child. You have brought me back my childhood. When I travel around the world on the seder night and people open their doors to me, I am often lonely. Now I will travel with my bird of clay and stone that is made from the mystery of prayer and time. If, on the seder night, I do not come right away when you welcome me in, you must know that I will be coming. Look outside in the street and see if there are any stone feathers glowing on the ground. If you see them, then I cannot be far away."

Then there was a sound of beating feathers and the bird grew and grew, and Elijah the Prophet sat upon it and flew away.

❖

For the rest of his life, Joseph the Potter kept a little stone feather in his smock and touched it for inspiration as he worked.

Every Pesach, when children all over Haifa opened their doors for Elijah and Elijah did not enter immediately, Joseph the Potter told them the story of how he had once met Elijah. Joseph showed them the stone feather and repeated Elijah's words, and the children did not worry.

"... If, on the seder night, I do not come right away when you welcome me in, you must know that I will be coming. Look outside on the street and see if there are any stone feathers glowing on the ground. If you see them, then I cannot be far away."

Glossary

ark n. (arc) derived from Latin. The sacred chest in which the ancient Hebrews kept the stone tablets containing the Ten Commandments. In modern times this refers to the cabinet where the Torah scrolls are kept in synagogues.

bar mitzvah n. (bar MITZ-va) Hebrew. A thirteen-year-old Jewish boy's formal entering into the adult Jewish community in honor of reaching the age of religious duty and responsibility. The experience for Jewish girls is called bat mitzvah.

Glossary

challah n. (CHAL-la, with the Scottish *ch* of *loch*)
challot n., pl. (chal-LOTE) Hebrew. The special braided Sabbath breadloaf.

Eliahu Ha-Novi n. (ay-lee-A-who ha-nuh-VEE) Hebrew. Elijah the Prophet. In the story "Leaves," this refers to the customary song about Elijah that the husband and wife sing after Shabbat.

haftarah n. (haf-TOE-ra) Hebrew. Reading from the Book of Prophets, following the Torah reading on Shabbat.

Haifa n. (HI-fa) Hebrew. Israel's largest Mediterranean seaport and third-largest city.

Hanukkah n. (HAN-na-ka) Hebrew. The eight-day holiday during which candles are lit each evening to commemorate the Maccabean victory over the Greek occupiers of Judea in 165 B.C.E. It is believed that the Maccabees found a jar of oil that could burn for only one day, but a miracle occurred

57

and the oil lasted eight days. Also called the Festival of Lights or the Festival of Rededication.

Havdalah n. (hav-DAH-la) Hebrew. The ceremony marking the separation of the Sabbath from the rest of the week.

Jerusalem n. (je-ROO-sa-lem) derived from Hebrew. An ancient holy city and a center of pilgrimage for Jews, Christians, and Muslims. The capital of ancient Israel and Judea from the time of King David until the destruction of the second Temple in 70 C.E. The capital of Israel since 1950.

kibbutz n. (key-BOOTS) **kibbutzim** n., pl. (key-boot-SEEM) Hebrew. Israeli communal farms; also industrial collective settlements.

kotel n. (CO-tell) Hebrew. The Western Wall, the only relic of the Jerusalem Temple of 2,000 years ago, the most sacred place on Earth to the Jewish people. Also known as the Wailing Wall.

Mashiach   n.   (mush-EE-ach, with the Scottish *ch* of *loch*)   Hebrew.   The Messiah, the redeemer of suffering for the Jewish people and, some believe, for the world.

menorah   n.   (muh-NOR-a)   Hebrew.   A candelabrum with nine branches: eight branches to commemorate the miracle of Hanukkah and one branch to hold the candle that is used to light the others.

mitzvah   n.   (MITZ-va)   Hebrew.   Commandment. A good deed done as a religious duty without any expectation of an earthly reward.

Pesach   n.   (PACE-ach, with the Scottish *ch* of *loch*) Hebrew.   The eight-day Jewish holiday of Passover, celebrating the Jewish deliverance from slavery in ancient Egypt.

rabbi   n.   (RAB-eye)   Hebrew.   An ordained teacher of the Jewish law. Also a spiritual leader of a synagogue.

sanctuary n. (SANK-choo-ary) derived from Late Latin. A holy place of prayer in a synagogue.

seder n. (SAY-dur) Hebrew. The ceremonial meal on the first and second nights of the Passover holiday, during which ritual foods are eaten and the story is told of the Jewish deliverance from slavery in ancient Egypt. In Israel, the seder is only held on the first night of Passover.

Shabbat n. (sha-BAT) Hebrew. The Jewish Sabbath, the day of rest from sundown Friday until nightfall on Saturday.

Shabbat Shalom! (sha-BAT sha-LOME) Hebrew. The customary pre-Sabbath and Sabbath greeting.

Shabbos n. (SHA-bus) Yiddish. Shabbat.

Shana tova (sha-NA toe-VA) Hebrew. "A good year" or "Happy New Year." It is the greeting on the High Holy Days, beginning with Rosh Hashanah, the Jewish New Year, and ending with Yom Kippur, the Day of Atonement.

Shana tova vi chaim tovim (sha-NA toe-VA vee cha-YEEM toe-VEEM, with the Scottish *ch* of *loch*) Hebrew. "A good year and a good life." This is part of Elijah's blessing to the young boy in the story "The Tallis."

siddur n. (see-DOOR) Hebrew. Prayer book.

Sleecha (slee-CHA, with the Scottish *ch* of *loch*) Hebrew. "Excuse me."

succah n. (soo-KA) **succot** n., pl. (soo-COAT) Hebrew. A hut roofed with branches built near a house or synagogue and used as a temporary dining or living area during Succot.

Succot n. (soo-COAT) Hebrew. The Festival of Booths. A harvest holiday that commemorates the temporary shelter used by Jews who were farmers in ancient times. The holiday also commemorates the fragile booths used by Jews when they were wandering in the desert after their Exodus from Egypt.

synagogue n. (SIN-a-gog) derived from Greek. The building or place of assembly used by Jewish communities primarily for religious worship.

tallis n. (TAL-lis) Hebrew. A Jewish prayer shawl.

Tel Aviv n. (TEL a-VEEVE) Hebrew. Israel's main metropolis.

Torah n. (TOE-ra) Hebrew. The five books of Moses. Also, the name of the scroll upon which the books are handwritten in Hebrew.

yarmulke n. (YAR-ma-ka) Yiddish. A skullcap often worn by Jews during prayer.

yeshiva n. (ye-SHEE-va) Hebrew. An Orthodox Jewish school of higher instruction in Jewish learning, mainly for students preparing to be rabbis.

Glossary

Also a traditional Jewish day school providing secular and religious instruction.

Yom Kippur n. (YOM kip-POOR) Hebrew. The Day of Atonement. A solemn day of the Jewish year reserved for fasting and prayer. It is believed that on this day, the fate of each Jewish person is decided for the coming year.

Sydelle Pearl

started writing stories and poems when she was eight years old. Today she is a professional storyteller. Originally from South Orange, New Jersey, she now lives in Brookline, Massachusetts.

Rossitza Skortcheva

has exhibited her work around the world. The illustrator of many children's books, she makes her home in Providence, Rhode Island.